A Pony Called Angel

Best

Rosie pulled at th

not going that way."

But Angel ignored her and carried on down the drive towards the stables. She broke into a trot.

"Rosie, stop her!" Rosie's mum cried. Rosie pulled as hard as she could but it made no difference. Ignoring Rosie's tugs on the reins, Angel pricked her ears and trotted determinedly down the drive!

Other Series by Linda Chapman

A Pony Called Angel

Best Friends

Linda Chapman

Best Friends (A Pony Called Angel Book 1)

Special thanks to Katie Collington, Milly Ellerton, Charlie Haynes and Bertie the pony who let me use their names; to Sue Collington for talking to me about sheep farming; to Amany Chapman, Iola Chapman and Julie Sykes for reading the story at an early stage and encouraging me; to Philippa Milnes-Smith for all her fantastic editorial comments and suggestions and most of all to our own Angel-pony who is just as pretty, clever, kind and cheeky as the Angel in this book!
L.C.

CHAPTER ONE

The end-of-school bell rang out. Miss Haynes raised her eyebrows, holding the class in their seats for a moment and then her face relaxed into a smile. "OK, everyone. Off you go. Have a lovely Easter holidays."

Rosie Collington's breath left her in a rush. The Easter holidays! Two weeks without any school; two weeks where she could go to the stables; two weeks where she could just hang around at home and be with animals all day long.

The rest of the class were shoving their chairs back, calling out to their friends. Rosie caught up with her best friend, Alice. "It's the holidays at last!"

Alice nodded. "I almost wish I wasn't going away. I'm going to miss staying at yours."

Alice usually spent the Easter holidays sleeping over at Rosie's house and helping out – Rosie lived on a sheep farm and it was always a very busy time of year for her family because it was when the lambs were born. However, this Easter, Alice was going to America.

"I'm going to miss you too," Rosie

told her as they got their coats. "But I'll email you lots of photos of the lambs and you can come and sleepover when you get back. If the weather's nice we can camp in the garden."

"Definitely!" said Alice. "I can bring us back loads of American sweets to eat."

Rosie's mum, Mrs Collington, came to the cloakroom door. "Come on, Rosie. We can't hang around today. I've got so much to do at home." Mrs Collington smiled at Alice. "Have a lovely holiday, Alice. Your mum says you're going to Disney World."

Alice nodded. "Just for a few days,

the rest of the time we're at my cousins' house. They've got their own swimming pool."

"Send me photos," said Rosie.

"I will," Alice promised.

"It's going to be strange not seeing Alice this holidays," Mrs Collington said to Rosie, as they walked to the car. "At least you've got Jack."

"Mmm," Rosie said, fiddling with the end of her long, blonde plait. "But Jack's not so much fun anymore." Her brother, Jack was twelve – a year older than her. When they had been younger they had played together lots but since Jack had started at secondary school he'd changed. Now, when he wasn't helping on the farm, he was always glued to his phone, or to the Xbox. "Maybe I could go to the riding stables?" she suggested. "They have pony days every Tuesday, Wednesday and Friday."

Her mum sighed. "Oh, sweetie, I'm sorry but those pony days are so expensive. I just don't think it's possible this holiday – money is really tight at the moment."

"Oh." Rosie's heart sank.

Her mum squeezed her arm. "Hopefully things will improve by the summer and you can go on some pony days then."

The summer felt like a long time away. Some of the excitement that had been fizzing inside Rosie at the thought of the Easter holidays faded slightly. She stared out of the window.

If only I had a pony of my own, she thought. *Then I could ride that.*

It was her big dream. She thought about it every day and she had it all planned out. The pony could live in one of the fields with the sheep and there was even an old stable in the farmyard that she could clean out and use. She just needed her dad to agree. But he didn't like ponies. *'Useless creatures. All they do is eat the grass and cut my fields up with their hooves,'* he always said whenever she asked.

Rosie thought about all the reasons why she should have a pony as her mum drove the rest of the way home. If only she could change her dad's mind!

Glebe Farm, where they lived, was about a mile outside of the village of Saxelby on a quiet country lane. The house was an old, red brick farmhouse with a white, rambling rose growing around the door. The large front garden was split in half by the driveway. On one side was an old wooden swing and on the other side four apple trees with yellow daffodils bobbing around the trunks. The farmyard was behind the house with the barns, hen pens, an old stone stable and tractors. Spread out behind the farmyard was a patchwork of fields, filled with white, woolly sheep.

When Rosie's mum had parked the car, Rosie ran inside, got changed and then went outside to help. There were water buckets to be filled and sheep pens that needed fresh straw. The new lambs bleated as they fed from their mothers, their little tails waggling.

After she had finished putting the straw in the pens, her mum asked her to walk round one the East Field, checking the hedges and fences. "Your dad's planning on putting some of the ewes and lambs out there tomorrow," she said. "We need to be sure there's no places they can

8

escape."

Rosie set off happily around the field. The spring sun warmed her bare arms and, breathing in the smell of the fresh green grass, she imagined she had three ponies of her own – a grey pony called Snowy, a black pony with white socks called Prince and a chestnut pony with a flaxen mane and tail called Swift. She pretended she was riding Prince, cantering him along the edge of the field.

Suddenly she noticed a gap in the hedge that separated their land from the neighbouring farm. It was quite a large hole, definitely big enough for a sheep to get through. She'd have to tell Dad about it. She knelt down to check it out.

"Oh!" she gasped in shock as she looked through. In the field, on the other side of the hedge, was a beautiful golden pony!

CHAPTER TWO

Seeing Rosie, the pony gave a friendly whicker. "Hello," Rosie breathed. She squeezed through the hole in the hedge. "What are you doing here?" The Stuarts who owned the fields that side of the hedge didn't have any horses and their children were grown up now.

The pony came over. She had a perfect white blaze, a long white forelock and a white tail that swept almost to the ground. She looked about thirteen hands high and her golden coat glowed in the sunlight. She nuzzled Rosie's hands then lifted her muzzle and snuffled at Rosie's hair.

Rosie giggled.

"Hello there, Rosie!" Rosie heard a man's voice. She looked round. Mr Stuart, the next-door farmer, was standing by the field gate.

"Hi, Mr Stuart!" Rosie called. She hurried across the field. The pony trotted after her as if she didn't want to be parted from her.

"I see you've met our new visitor," Mr Stuart said as Rosie stopped by the gate and the pony stopped beside her. "She's a friendly little thing, isn't she?"

"Who does she belong to? Why's she here? How long is she staying?" The words tumbled out of Rosie.

"She belongs to my niece, Meghan," said Mr Stuart as the pony nudged at Rosie's pockets with her nose, trying to find some treats. "Meg's outgrown her now and is going to study overseas but she couldn't bear to sell her so she asked us if she could come and stay with us so she could still visit her when she's back. I said I'd happily have her to stay – I've always liked ponies."

"So, she's going to live here?" Rosie's voice rose as an amazing, wonderful idea started to rise up inside her like a wave swelling in the ocean.

Mr Stuart nodded.

"Would you ..." Rosie could hardly speak for excitement. "Would you like someone to look after and groom her and maybe even *ride* her, Mr Stuart?"

A smile slowly creased up Mr Stuart's weather-beaten face. "And who would that someone be?"

"Me!" Rosie exclaimed. "Well, if Mum and Dad say it's OK," she added hastily.

Mr Stuart considered it. "I don't see why not. She has all her tack and bits and pieces and her hooves have just been trimmed so there'll be no big expense for your mum and dad. I'm sure Meg would be happy to know Angel was being looked after and loved."

"Angel?" Rosie repeated.

"Aye. That's her name."

"Angel," Rosie breathed, stroking the pony. It was the most perfect name. Angel pushed against Rosie with her nose.

Rosie felt excitement surge through her. "Oh, Mr Stuart! Let me go and ask Mum straight away!"

Before Mr Stuart could say another word, she had turned and ran back across the field with Angel cantering eagerly beside her all the way.

*

"Slow down, Rosie," Mrs Collington said ten minutes later. Darwin, the black and white cat, was snoozing on the tiled floor beside the old cream Aga and there was the delicious smell of lasagna baking in the oven. "Get your breath back and start again. There's a pony? Where?"

Rosie had been so out of breath as she ran through the back door that she had barely been able to gasp out anything other than "Angel... pony... in the field... *please!*"

Rosie gulped in a lungful of air and then told her mum what had just happened. "She's called Angel and Mr Stuart says I can help look after her if you and Dad say that's OK," she finished in a rush. She hopped from foot to foot. "She's got all her tack and everything so she won't cost you anything. Please, please, please, Mum! I could go over there every day and see her."

Her mum rubbed her hands over her eyes. "Oh, Rosie, I don't know. Life's so busy. I just can't take anything more on at the moment."

Rosie looked at her desperately. "I'll do anything. I'll help on the farm as much as you like."

Her mum studied her face for a moment and her eyes softened. "Well, maybe it wouldn't be too much extra hassle."

"Really?" Rosie gasped.

Her mum nodded. "If the Stuarts say the pony's safe to ride and your dad agrees then yes, you can look after her. We could even ask the Stuarts if she could move into one of our fields. I'd feel happier if you weren't bothering the Stuarts by going round there every day."

Rosie hugged her mum. "Oh, thank you! Thank you!"

"Don't get too excited yet, we have to convince Dad and you know his view on ponies," her mum warned.

Just then there was the sound of Mr Collington's truck pulling into the farmyard. "He's here!" Rosie exclaimed, her eyes widening.

"Let me talk to him first," said her

mum.

Rosie ran outside. Nell, the brown-and-white sheepdog, jumped out of the truck and Jack and her dad followed. Rosie raced over to them. "Come inside, Dad. There's something Mum needs to talk to you about."

Nell jumped around, sensing Rosie's excitement.

"What's the rush?" Mr Collington said in surprise.

"It's important." Rosie grabbed his hand. "Oh, I love you so much, Dad. I really, really do!"

Her dad gave her a suspicious look. "OK. What do you want, Rosie Posie?"

"Rosie!" her mum called warningly from the back door. "Let me talk to your dad first. Come in, love. The kettle's on."

Mr Collington went inside. Rosie watched him. She crossed her fingers tightly. *Oh please, please, please say yes*, she prayed.

CHAPTER THREE

"What's going on?" Jack asked. He had the same thick blonde hair and blue eyes as Rosie but his hair was cut short.

Rosie told him about Angel.

Jack frowned. "A pony? Why do you want a pony? It'll just be extra work."

"But lots of extra fun too," said Rosie.

Jack gave Rosie a look that plainly

said he thought she was nuts. "I'd rather be playing on the X-box."

"Yes, but I'd rather be with a pony," she told him.

He shook his head. "You're weird."

"No, I'm not!"

"Dad will never say yes anyway," Jack told her.

"He might," Rosie said hopefully.

She hurried inside. What was happening? Her dad was sitting at the table with a cup of tea. Her heart plummeted as she heard him saying, "Oh no, Sal. Definitely not. It's just one more animal to feed and water. I'm not having it."

"But Rosie will look after her," Mrs

Collington said.

"I will, Dad!" Rosie jumped in eagerly. "I promise I will. You won't have to do anything. I know loads about ponies. I've been learning to ride since I was five!" She clasped her hands together. "Please, I want this more than anything in the world." She looked at him beseechingly.

To her disappointment, her dad shook his head.

"But Pete, Rosie is such a good help on the farm," her mum said. "I'm sure she's responsible enough to look after a pony now and I can help her if she needs it. I always wanted a pony when I was younger. I'd love to have one here and this one will hardly cost us anything. It's like it was meant to be."

Rosie's dad hesitated, his expression torn. "Well, yes, but..."

"How about we try it out for the next two weeks?" Mrs Collington said persuasively. "Just over the Easter holidays. Think of it as if we're just borrowing her for a while. If it's not working out then we tell the Stuarts and they can have her back."

Mr Collington considered it. "I guess two weeks isn't too long. We can see if Rosie is still as keen on all the looking after when she's been doing it every day for two weeks."

"I will be!" Rosie told him, excitement surging up inside. "Oh, thank you! Thank you!" She hugged him tightly.

"It's just a trial," he reminded them. "She's not yours. Remember that. It's just for Easter. She's more than likely going back after that."

But Rosie ignored his warning. She twirled around the room making Nell bark. A picture of the beautiful golden pony filled her head.

Oh, Angel, she thought in delight. *We're going to have so much fun together!*

Mrs Collington rang the Stuarts. Mr Stuart reassured Mrs Collington that Angel was very well behaved and good to ride and said he was happy for Angel to live in one of the

Collington's fields. He offered to bring her round to the farmhouse so that Rosie could try her out and see if she was suitable. While Rosie was waiting she rang Alice – she couldn't wait to tell her – but there was no reply. She waited five minutes and then rang her again but still no reply. In the end, she used her mum's ipad to send Alice a message instead:

OMG! Guess what? I've got a pony!! Only 4 2 wks at moment but I'm gonna make Dad let me keep her. Can't wait for u to c her. Xxx ps she's called Angel!!!

Alice liked animals – she wanted to be a vet – but she wasn't as pony-mad as Rosie was. However, Rosie knew that Alice would understand what a big deal it was.

She went outside and stared at the driveway, willing Mr Stuart to arrive. Every second seemed to drag but at last she saw him coming along the road, leading Angel and carrying a grooming kit. Angel was tacked up. Rosie guessed he had put the saddle and bridle on her to save carrying them round himself. She ran to meet him.

"I see you persuaded your dad to give it a try then, lass?" Mr Stuart said with a smile.

Rosie nodded. "I'm so happy!" she told him.

Angel snorted and rubbed her head against Rosie's arm.

"Looks like you're not the only one," said Mr Stuart with a chuckle and he let Rosie lead Angel the rest of the way down the drive.

Her mum and dad came out of the house. "She's very pretty," Rosie's mum said.

"She looks like a pony to me," said Rosie's dad gruffly. "Four feet, a mouth, eats a lot I'm sure."

Mr Stuart patted Angel. "You take good care of Rosie now, Angel."

Angel studied him with her ears pricked.

The two men went off and Rosie and Mum took Angel to the Home

Field – the closest field to the yard. "Dad said you can keep her in here. It'll save you carrying your tack and grooming kit too far. You can keep them in the old stable," her mum said. "Now, go and get your hat and let's see what she's like to ride."

Rosie ran inside to get her riding hat and then her mum held Angel, while Rosie mounted and adjusted her stirrups. Nerves fluttered in her tummy. She didn't think she could bear it if Angel was naughty and her mum said they couldn't keep her. She touched Angel's golden neck.

"Walk on," she whispered. Angel set off around the field. She moved with quick, eager steps. At first Rosie felt tense in the saddle, wondering if she was going to break into a trot or a canter but Angel stayed at a walk. Rosie circled her and then asked her to halt and rein back. Angel did everything Rosie asked her to. Feeling braver, Rosie touched her heels to Angel's sides. "Trot on!"

Angel moved into a steady trot. Rosie rose up and down. She started to smile as she changed direction and rode in circles. Angel was so good! It was like she could read her mind. The pony went faster at the slightest touch of Rosie's legs but slowed down as soon as Rosie pulled the reins. Rosie finished by cantering around the field and then stopped by her mum, a huge beam on her face.

"I love her," she said, hugging Angel's neck. "She's perfect, Mum!"

Mrs Collington stroked Angel's nose. "Be as good as that everyday for Rosie and I'll think you're perfect too."

Angel rubbed her nose against her. Mrs Collington chuckled. "OK, Rosie. She's yours at least until the end of the holidays. After that, well, we'll just have to see what your dad says."

CHAPTER FOUR

After supper, Rosie checked her mum's ipad. There was a message from Alice.

That's soooooo cool! Can't wait to c Angel when I get back. You're soooooo lucky. Wish I could come over 2moro and c her instead of going on a plane! Xxx

Rosie smiled and sent a message back.

I wish u cd 2!! I'll send u pics! X

Rosie put the ipad down and got ready for bed. As she snuggled down, she thought about Angel. They would go out for rides and canter round the fields, maybe even do a few little jumps – all the things Rosie had always imagined doing if she had her own pony. Smiling happily, she fell asleep.

*

"Can one of you to go and check the hedges in the Hill Field this morning please?" Mr Collington said the next day as Rosie and Jack ate breakfast. They had already been up and out on the farm, helping to sweep the barn, refill water buckets and cleaning out the pens that had been used in the night. The sheep would stay in them for a little while longer while the ewes were wormed and the lambs' coats marked with a number written in dye so that Mr and Mrs Collington would know which sheep belonged to which ewe. Rosie had managed to spend a few minutes hugging Angel but that was all she had allowed herself. She definitely didn't want her mum and dad thinking she was going to work less hard on the farm just because she had a pony to look after.

"I don't mind checking the field," Rosie offered. "I can ride Angel round it, it'll be much quicker that way."

Her dad considered it. "I guess that's not such a bad idea. If we've got to keep a pony, it might as well make itself useful."

After breakfast, Rosie got Angel ready. Just as she finished tacking up, it started to rain. Rosie didn't care though. A bit of rain wasn't going to stop her riding! She mounted and rode Angel to the end of the driveway. Looking carefully left and right she crossed the quiet road and rode up to the first gate that led into Hill Field. She managed to open and close it without having to dismount. Angel even helped by pushing the gate open and shut with her nose!

"You're so clever," Rosie told her. "OK, let's check these hedges." They set off. The rain was getting heavier now, the drops splashing on to Rosie's jodhpurs.

Angel pricked her ears and peered at something in the distance then she broke into a trot. Rosie grabbed at the slippery reins. "Steady, girl!"

But Angel ignored Rosie and broke into a canter. Rosie lost a stirrup and grabbed a handful of mane. "Stop, Angel!" she gasped. "I'm falling off!"

Angel slowed down. Rosie hauled herself back into the saddle and picked up the reins. But the second she had her balance back Angel was off again. Her eyes were fixed on a point halfway up the field where several sheep were clustered around the hedge that separated the field from the road.

"Whoa, Angel!" Rosie cried. "What are you doing?"

Angel reached the sheep and stopped.

"Angel!" said Rosie breathlessly, her heart pounding. "You mustn't take off like that."

Lowering her head, Angel stared at the hedge.

Rosie suddenly realised what Angel was looking at – and why the sheep were gathered around the hedge. Although the branches were had a barrier of metal sheep wire in front of them, the wire had been pushed up at one point making a sheep-sized hole. On the other side of the hedge, a ewe and a black-faced lamb were now standing on the grass verge near the road.

"Oh no," Rosie breathed.

She scrambled off Angel's back and pulled the wire back down to stop any other sheep getting out. Then she weighted it down with a big rock and quickly remounted. Now she had to do something about the ewe and lamb on the other side!

She got back on Angel and they trotted to where there was another gate that led on to the road. As they went through it, the lamb started wandering on to the tarmac. "Oh no, don't do that," said Rosie desperately, kicking Angel on.

"Maaaa!" the lamb said in its high-pitched voice and then bounced away down the centre of the road, its tiny hooves splashing through the puddles.

Its mother followed. Rosie let Angel trot after them, herding them down the road towards the farm's driveway. If she could get them in there then they would be safe. The rain hit her face. Anxiety welled inside her. If a car came the road might be too slippery for it to stop in time. It might hit the lamb, or ewe – or even her and Angel. She knew she shouldn't be out there on the road on her own but she had to try and do something. "Come on, Angel!" she urged.

Rosie froze as she heard the roar of a car's engine. Glancing over her shoulder, she saw a black car speeding towards them round the bend.

She waved her arms frantically to slow the car down.

The driver hit his brakes. For one horrible moment, Rosie thought the car wasn't going to be able to stop but Angel jumped forwards and the car skidded to a halt just a few inches away from her. Rosie grabbed Angel's mane thinking Angel might be scared and gallop off but the pony didn't turn a hair. She just snorted rather crossly at the car and then continued to trot after the sheep and herded them into the driveway.

Rosie swung round in the saddle. The driver had jumped out of his car. "Are you OK?" he asked her anxiously.

"I'm fine," she called back. She could see her dad coming up the drive in his truck. "My dad's on his way," Rosie said, pointing. "He'll be able to help me with the sheep."

The driver looked relieved and got back into his car. He had just driven off when her dad stopped his truck and leapt out with Nell at his heels.

"Whatever's going on, Rosie?" he exclaimed. "What are you doing out on the roads on your own? And why are these sheep out?" He looked angry. "I knew having a pony would be nothing but trouble."

"Dad! It's not Angel's fault. She's been amazing!" Rosie explained what had happened. "She herded the lamb and sheep all the way back here. And she was the one who noticed there was something wrong when we first went into the field – she took me to the gap in the hedge."

The anger slowly faded from her dad's face. "Well, I don't think ponies are quite that clever," he said skeptically. "But the important thing is you're all safe. You really shouldn't have come out on the roads on your own but well done for saving the ewe and lamb. I hope that driver's learnt a lesson and drives more slowly on these lanes in future."

Mr Collington whistled to Nell. She started rounding up the lamb and ewe who were grazing on the grass at the edge of the driveway. "I'll get these two back in the field and fix that fence. Can you tell Mum where I am?"

Rosie nodded and rode Angel down the drive. Her mind was buzzing. Her dad might think that ponies weren't clever but it was like Angel had known there was trouble and set out to deal with it. She leant down and hugged Angel's neck.

"Dad can say what he likes but I think you really *are* that clever, aren't you?" Rosie whispered.

Angel tossed her head in reply.

CHAPTER FIVE

"Can I take Angel out on a hack today?" Rosie asked the next morning.

"Not today, sweetheart," her mum said. "I'll need to come with you if you want to go on the roads and I've got too much on."

"Just a short ride, Mum," Rosie begged. "Please."

"I really can't," her mum said. "I've got to get the beef into the slow cooker for supper tonight, order some more fencing and sort the washing when it's done."

"I'll sort the washing out later for you," said Rosie. "Please can we go?"

Her mum gave in. "Oh, all right then. As long as you *do* help me. Go and get her ready."

Rosie ran down to the field. Angel whinnied when she saw her coming and Rosie's heart sang with delight.

She tied Angel up. As she groomed, she told Angel all about Alice. "She's my best friend, Angel," she said. "She's in America at the moment but you'll really like her when you meet her."

If Dad lets you stay. Rosie quickly

pushed the thought away. She couldn't bear it if her dad sent Angel back to the Stuarts after the holidays. Angel just had to carry on being as good and clever as she had been the day before.

"Alice and I have been best friends since we started at primary school," Rosie went on. "But we'll be going to different schools in September when we move to secondary school. It's going to be weird."

Angel's ears flickered as if she was listening. Rosie carried on talking, telling her how she and Alice had promised they would be best friends forever, but how she also hoped she'd make new friends at her new school.

It was so nice being able to talk to Angel and she was sure Angel liked it too. "I'd love to make friends with someone who's as pony-mad as me at my new school. Alice gets bored if I talk about ponies too much," she said.

When she finished grooming, Rosie fetched Angel's tack. She had undone all the buckles the night before to give it a proper clean. She hoped she'd put it all back together properly. The bridle had been a bit difficult but when she put it on it seemed to fit. Rosie put some hoof oil on Angel's hooves and then stood back to admire her. She looked lovely with her shining hooves, golden coat and clean tack.

"Pity about me," Rosie muttered ruefully, looking down at her jodhpurs which were now covered with hair, mud and grease from grooming.

Angel tossed her head and pushed the side of her face against Rosie. "Do you want a cuddle?" Rosie said.

Angel pushed even harder, almost knocking Rosie over. "Angel, stop it!" Rosie giggled.

Angel pushed at her again, rubbing her bridle against Rosie's arm.

Just then Mrs Collington came out of the house with her walking shoes on. "All ready? On you hop then."

Angel threw her head up and

down making her bridle jingle as Rosie mounted.

"Don't be naughty, Angel!" Mrs Collington said, giving her a sharp tap on the neck.

Angel put her ears back.

"Now you've upset her, Mum," said Rosie. She bent down and hugged Angel's neck. "Don't worry. I don't think you're naughty." Angel rubbed her muzzle against Rosie's knee.

Rosie smiled and straightened up. "Walk on then," she said. Angel huffed but then walked out quietly through the gate.

They went up the drive and headed along the road towards the next village, Keysall. A large tractor rumbled past but Angel didn't even flinch. As they walked along the road, Rosie and her mum chatted about the farm and school. It was odd just being the two of them and having chance to chat without her mum trying to do other things at the same time but Rosie really liked it.

After about ten minutes, Angel lifted her head and whinnied. They were approaching some fields with horses in. Rosie knew the fields were owned by Orchard Stables. It was a small riding school and livery yard that had just started up eight months ago. Although it was close to Glebe Farm, Rosie didn't have riding lessons there because her mum had wanted her to stay at Hill Top Stables – the large riding school where her mum had learned to ride when she was little.

The horses and ponies in the fields came trotting over to the hedge. Angel stopped and sniffed noses with them. When Rosie tried to make her walk on, Angel whinnied to her new friends and tried to turn down the driveway that led to the stables instead.

Rosie pulled at the reins. "No, Angel. We're not going that way."

But Angel ignored her and carried on down the drive towards the stables. She broke into a trot.

"Rosie, stop her!" Mrs Collington cried.

Rosie pulled as hard as she could but it made no difference. Ignoring Rosie's tugs on the reins, Angel pricked her ears and trotted determinedly down the drive!

CHAPTER SIX

"Hang on, Rosie!" Mrs Collington shouted.

Rosie hauled on the reins. "Whoa, Angel! Stop!"

At the end of the drive there was a stableyard with two barns with a big schooling arena in front of them. A woman with red hair was cantering a chestnut horse around the arena and there were people on the yard, grooming ponies and pushing wheelbarrows. Hearing the sound of

Angel's hooves, they all looked round. Angel skidded in through the gateway and halted.

Rosie's cheeks were on fire. She saw two teenagers on the yard nudging each other and giggling as they pointed at her.

A girl came hurrying over. She was small – at first Rosie thought she must be about eight but as she got closer Rosie saw that she looked older, maybe the same age as her. She had brown hair that curled under at her chin, thick dark eyebrows and eyes the colour of milk chocolate. "Are you OK?" she asked anxiously.

"I'm… I'm fine. Angel – my pony – just took off down the driveway. I don't know why." Rosie glanced round. Her mum was running down the driveway after her. "Oh help, I'm going to be in so much trouble," she groaned, her heart sinking.

The lady who had been riding in the arena led her horse over. Her red hair was tied back in a short ponytail and she had freckles. Rosie found it hard to guess adults' ages but she guessed the lady was probably about thirty. "Are you all right? What happened?" she called.

Rosie's cheeks burned an even deeper red. "I'm fine. I'm sorry. I was out for a hack and my pony took off with me down your drive."

The lady gave her a friendly smile.

"Ponies! They can be so naughty!"

Rosie felt a bit better. She'd been expecting to be told off.

"Is this your mum?" the lady asked.

Rosie nodded as her mum came running up to them. "I'm so sorry," Mrs Collington panted. "We didn't mean to disturb you."

"It doesn't matter at all. I'm Hayley. I own these stables," the lady said.

"I know. I think we met just after you first moved in here. I'm Sally Collington and this is my daughter, Rosie. We live at Glebe Farm, just down the road."

Hayley smiled. "Of course! I

thought I recognized you. Nice to meet you again."

"I really am sorry if we disturbed you. Rosie's only been riding Angel for a couple of days," Mrs Collington explained. "She's been so good up until now."

Well, apart from when she took off yesterday in the field, Rosie thought. But she didn't say anything because she was secretly sure Angel had done that because she knew the sheep were in danger.

"She looks like a nice pony," said Hayley. "And just the right size for you, Rosie."

"She's perfect," said Rosie.

Angel nodded as if she agreed.

Hayley chuckled. "So, where do you normally ride?"

"Hill Top Equestrian Centre," Rosie said.

"That's a good riding stables. It might be an idea to try and have some lessons there on Angel," said Hayley. "Lovely though she seems to be, you don't want her to get cheeky and think she can trot off with you whenever she likes."

"Unfortunately we don't have a horse trailer," said Rosie's mum. She looked round thoughtfully. "But, you're right, it would be good for Rosie to have a few lessons on Angel. Do you think you would be able to fit her in here for a lesson at some point,

Hayley?"

Rosie caught her breath in delight. It would be really fun to have lessons on Angel! Angel seemed to feel the same. She stamped a front hoof eagerly.

"Of course I can," said Hayley. "I do private lessons or the cheaper option is for Rosie to join in with one of my regular rides. My intermediate group is having a lesson in half an hour. Most of the girls in that are about Rosie's age. If you want to, you could join in with that?" she said, looking at Rosie. "We're doing some jumping. Do you like jumping?"

"Oh, yes," Rosie said eagerly. "I love it although I haven't jumped

Angel yet."

"Well, a lesson would be the perfect place to try her out," said Hayley.

"Can I, Mum?" Rosie turned to her mum.

Her mum hesitated. "I can't really hang round here all morning, Rosie."

"If you want, a couple of the older girls can hack back home with Rosie after the lesson," Hayley said to Rosie's mum. "That would save you hanging round."

"Really? Well, that would be fantastic if you don't mind," Mrs Collington said.

"Not at all. I'll just need you to fill in some forms for insurance purposes," Hayley said. "Milly, can you show Rosie round? Angel can go in one of the pony stables for now."

"Sure." Milly flashed a grin at Rosie. "Come this way!"

Rosie dismounted and led Angel after Milly.

"You're really lucky to have a pony of your own," Milly said to her.

"She isn't exactly mine. I'm just kind of borrowing her." Rosie explained to Milly how she had ended up looking after Angel for the Easter holidays. "Though I hope Dad says I can keep her after that," she finished.

"Oh, wow! You're so lucky. I wish something like that would happen to me," said Milly enviously as Angel nuzzled her.

"I still can't believe it," Rosie admitted, stroking Angel's nose. "I've wanted a pony forever."

"Me too," said Milly.

They smiled at each other. "So how long have you been riding here?" Rosie asked.

"Since Hayley opened the yard in August," said Milly. "I started off just coming for lessons but when I was eleven in November, Hayley said I could help in return for rides. My sister, Helena, helps too. She's thirteen. We live just across the fields so it's really easy for us to walk here."

"Where do you go to school?"

Rosie asked curiously.

"In Keysall."

Rosie nodded. That explained why she didn't know Milly. "I go to Saxelby. I'm going to Riverside Academy in September."

"So am I," Milly said. Her brown eyes lit up. "Hey, we might be in the same form. I hope so! I really want to make some friends who like ponies."

Rosie nodded eagerly. "Me too."

They left Angel in one of the stables while Milly showed Rosie round the yard. There was a barn for the horses and a barn for the ponies. Milly explained that some of the horses were liveries who belonged to other people, the rest were owned by

Hayley. She had two eventers and some young horses as well as ten horses and ponies she used in the riding school.

"Solo – who you just saw Hayley riding – is her top eventer," said Milly. "She does lots of competitions with him. He's a brilliant jumper – he never refuses a jump. Sometimes Helena and I go and watch her compete. We've got a cross-country course here and sometimes we have lessons on it. I love cross-country! And jumping!" The words bubbled out of her. "Come and see the jumping field. It's great!"

Milly showed Rosie all around the yard and then started introducing her to the horses and ponies.

"This is Pasco, he belongs to my sister's friend, Jo and this is Billy, he's the most chilled pony ever and Chimes who is Hayley's old mounted games pony…"

There were too many names to remember. Rosie was just patting Magpie, a piebald gelding who Milly said was her favourite because he was loved going fast when two teenagers came into the barn. They were pushing each other and laughing. One had dark hair with a fringe that slanted across her hazel eyes and thick eyebrows like Milly. The other had dark blonde hair caught up in a messy high ponytail and wide blue eyes.

"Who are you?" the blonde girl said, catching sight of Rosie.

"This is Rosie. Rosie this is Jo and my sister, Helena," said Milly.

"Hi," Rosie said, smiling.

Jo's eyes widened. "You're the one with that palomino pony! The pony that carted you down the driveway."

"Maybe she brought you here because she knew you needed some lessons!" Helena said. Both older girls sniggered.

Rosie blushed.

Jo gave Rosie an appraising look. "Did you know your ears stick out?"

Helena giggled.

Rosie put her hand to her ears.

They did stick out but only a tiny bit.

"Just ignore them," Milly said, glaring at the older girls. "They're really rude and annoying."

"Bye, Midget. Bye, Dumbo!" said Helena, wiggling her fingers as Rosie and Milly walked past them.

She and Jo cracked up laughing.

Milly and Rosie got out of the barn, the sounds of the hoots of laughter still ringing in their ears. "I'm sorry about that," Milly said, frowning back at the barn. "Ever since Helena turned thirteen she's been driving me mad. My little sister, Abigail is cute – she's six – but Helena is so annoying at the moment!"

"My older brother Jack can be really annoying too," said Rosie. "He just ignores me or teases me when his friends are round at ours."

"I know *all* about that!" said Milly with feeling. "Helena does that and her latest thing is playing a games of dares with Jo. They keep daring each other to do stupid things. Yesterday, Jo dared Helena to stand up on Magpie's back and the day before Helena dared Jo to ride her horse, Pasco, facing backwards. One of them's going to get hurt but when I tell them to stop, they won't listen."

They had just started talking about all the irritating things that older brothers and sisters did when Hayley came over. "You two look like you need a job," said Hayley, coming over. "Can you bring Fudge and Bertie in? If you take their bridles then you can ride them back."

Rosie and Milly walked up the drive and caught the two ponies: Fudge – a golden dun with a black mane and tail – and Bertie – a bay Exmoor pony with a pale-coloured muzzle.

"We're allowed to ride down the drive but never in the fields. It's too dangerous," Milly explained as they used the gate to get on to the ponies' backs. "All it takes is for one of the horses in the field to start cantering and then they might all start to stampede and it would be really dangerous to be riding one of them if they did that…" She broke off. "What are Jo and Helena doing now? Look! I bet it is another of their stupid dares."

She pointed to a field on the left further down the lane. It had a herd of young cows in, all with short sharp horns. Helena was standing beside the fence and Jo was climbing over it.

"The bullocks chase you if you go in that field. Hayley always tells us to walk the long way round and not cut through it if we have to catch one of the horses in the far field," Milly kicked Fudge into a trot.

Rosie kicked Bertie on too. He was a nice little pony but she wished she was riding Angel. Bertie's trot was much slower and he didn't read her mind like Angel did.

"What are you doing, Jo?" shouted Milly. "Stop!"

But Jo ignored her. Grinning at Helena, she dropped down on the other side of the fence and set off across the field at a run.

The nearest bullock lifted its head. It started walking towards her. The others noticed and started walking towards her too. Jo was halfway across the field now. The bullocks broke into a trot. They stared to canter straight at her. Rosie's breath caught in her throat. Their horns were small but looked very sharp and what if they knocked Jo over and trampled on her?

"She's not going to make it!" gasped Milly as the bullocks stampeded towards Jo.

Rosie's heart turned a somersault.

"Go on, Jo!" cried Helena. "Run!"

CHAPTER SEVEN

Jo sprinted for the fence on the far side and threw herself at it. She clambered over the top bar just as the bullocks reached it. They skidded to a halt, shaking their horns and scraping at the ground with their front hooves. She grinned from the other side of the fence and gave Helena, Rosie and Milly a thumbs up.

"She did it!" whooped Helena.

"You two are crazy," said Milly,

turning on Helena. "She could have got hurt."

"Oh, chill, Mill," said Helena. "Why don't you and your new little munchkin friend just go away and leave us alone?"

Milly scowled and kicked Fudge on. Rosie headed after her.

"They are *so* dumb," Milly muttered.

Rosie nodded. It had been a really stupid thing to do.

"One of them *is* going to get hurt soon," said Milly. "I want to tell on them but I can't. I just can't."

Rosie understood. She and Jack had an agreement that neither would ever tell tales about the other to their parents. You just didn't do that. No matter what the other one was doing. "Maybe they'll stop playing the game soon?" she said hopefully.

"Maybe," Milly said. She didn't sound like she thought it was likely though.

*

Back at the stables they helped tack up all the other ponies who were being used in the lesson. Rosie met some of the other teenage helpers on the yard including Kate who was eighteen and worked for Hayley full time. They were all friendly and they didn't tease her like Helena and Jo.

When the riding school ponies were ready and people were starting to arrive, Rosie went to get Angel ready. Angel whinnied and Rosie cuddled her for a few wonderful moments. It had been fun being with the other ponies but none of them were as beautiful – or clever – as Angel.

She fetched the tack from outside the stable. Hayley was walking up the aisle. "Do you need a hand, Rosie or can you get her tacked up on your own?" she asked.

"I can manage on my own, thanks," said Rosie.

"Great." Hayley looked puzzled as her eyes fell on the bridle. "Just a second," she said as Rosie started towards the stable door with it. "Can

I see your bridle?"

Rosie handed it to her in surprise. Why did Hayley want to see it?

"Your bit is on back to front," said Hayley. She pushed the bit rings together and showed Rosie how the two metal sides of the bit that went into Angel's mouth didn't meet as they should. "It'll hurt Angel if you ride with it like that. Did you put the bit on to the bridle like this?"

It was tempting to lie but Rosie didn't. "Yes," she whispered, feeling awful. "I must have put it on wrong when I cleaned my tack last night." Her cheeks were hot with embarrassment. "I didn't realise. But I think Angel did," she remembered.

"She kept nudging me this morning when I put her bridle on. I think she was trying to tell me something was wrong." She waited for Hayley to tell her off but Hayley just started undoing the buckles and changing the bit around.

"Never mind. It's an easy mistake to make. I'm impressed you gave your tack such a thorough clean that you took it all apart. Don't worry about it. Just make sure it's on the right way from now on. It's lucky Angel brought you here today or it might have been a while before someone spotted it. Aren't you a clever pony? Did you know you needed someone to sort it out?" She gave Angel a pat and hurried off.

Rosie let herself into the stable. "Oh, Angel, I'm so sorry," she said, feeling really guilty. Angel put her muzzle up to Rosie's face and nuzzled her cheek as if telling her it didn't matter.

Rosie remembered how Angel had rubbed her face against her that morning after she'd put the bridle on and how she'd tossed her head around until Rosie's mum had told her off. "I bet that *was* your way of trying to tell us the bit wasn't right, wasn't it?" she murmured. "I should have listened to you."

She put the bridle on and checked and rechecked every buckle. She didn't want to make any more mistakes. She was feeling nervous enough about the lesson as it was.

"Please be good," she said, kissing Angel's forehead. "I really like it here and I don't want Milly and Hayley to think I'm rubbish."

Angel blew out softly. As Rosie breathed in the sweet scent of Angel's breath, she felt her nerves calm down. It would be OK. She knew Angel wouldn't let her down.

"And I won't let you down again," she said, hugging her hard. "Next time you try and tell me something, I absolutely promise I'll listen. Is everything OK with your tack now?"

Angel snorted contentedly.

Rosie smiled.

*

"Excellent, Rosie! Good girl!"

Rosie glowed in delight as Angel jumped the last jump perfectly. The lesson was going brilliantly – Angel was doing everything she asked and Hayley was very encouraging and praised them whenever they did anything well.

"It looks like Angel really enjoys jumping," said Hayley coming over and patting her. "You're going to have a lot of fun with her."

Rosie beamed.

They all walked round on loose reins to cool the ponies down. Milly rode up alongside Rosie. "Angel was brilliant. Are you going to come for more lessons here?"

Rosie nodded. "Definitely. I wish I could come back again tomorrow!"

Hayley overheard and laughed. "That's what I like to hear. You're more than welcome to come back and help any day you want, Rosie. We've got a lead-rein pony day tomorrow and I always need helpers then. Usually people get a ride in exchange for helping but I'm happy if you want to bring Angel over and join in with what the other helpers are doing. If you fancy it ask your mum to give me a ring. Now, wait here and I'll go and get Helena and Jo to ride back with you."

Milly turned to Rosie as Hayley went over to the fence. "Oh, *please* start helping here! If you do, you'll be able to join in the helpers' Easter Egg hunt at the end of the holidays. We're going to go out on a ride to find a load of cut-out Easter eggs that Hayley has hidden and the winners – the first team back – get a huge Easter egg to share, then afterwards we'll all have a big barbecue."

"That sounds brilliant fun," said Rosie.

"It will be." Milly lowered her voice. "And if you come back, you can help me think of a way to stop Helena and Jo doing their stupid dares!"

"I'll try my best to persuade my mum," Rosie promised.

"See you tomorrow, I hope," said Milly, holding up crossed fingers as Helena and Jo appeared leading two horses.

Rosie felt a bit anxious about the ride home. She hoped Jo and Helena wouldn't start do anything stupid while she was with them or start teasing her again but to her relief they just ignored her, riding alongside each other and chatting as she rode behind on Angel.

Her mum came out of the house as they all rode up to the house. "Thanks for bringing Rosie home, girls," she said.

"No problem," Jo and Helena chorused politely.

Rosie had noticed over the morning how Jo and Helena changed around adults – they were always polite and well behaved then.

"See you soon, Rosie," said Jo. "It's been nice meeting you."

"Yeah, bye!" said Helena. They rode off.

"What lovely girls," Rosie's mum said.

Rosie wondered what her mum would say if she knew the truth. But right now she had more important things to think about. Jumping off Angel she told her mum what Hayley had said about her helping.

Her mum considered it. "It sounds like a good idea. It would be great for you to have some extra lessons on Angel."

"Lessons you don't have to pay for," Rosie added.

"Even better!" her mum said with a smile. "So, how's Angel been?"

"Perfect," said Rosie, stroking Angel's neck. "I don't know why she took off earlier."

"She was probably just being cheeky," said her mum. "Why don't you untack her and then come in and have some lunch?"

Mrs Collington went inside leaving Rose and Angel alone. "I'm very glad you did trot off with me," Rosie murmured. "I never would have gone to Orchard Stables if you hadn't. And we're going to have loads of fun there, Angel." She hugged her. "I just know we are!"

CHAPTER EIGHT

Rosie's mum walked Rosie and Angel up to the stables after breakfast the next day. As they headed up the road, Rosie told her mum all about the people and the ponies she had met the day before.

When Rosie rode on to the yard, Milly came running over. "You're back!"

Mrs Collington smiled. "You must be Milly. Rosie's told me lots about you."

Rosie cringed. Now, Milly would think she was weird or something but Milly just smiled even more widely. "I told my mum all about Rosie too," she confessed making Rosie feel much better. "It was really nice having someone else my age here. All the other girls who help are much older. I'm really glad Rosie's come back today."

Just then Hayley came over. "Hi, Rosie. Why don't you put Angel out in the small paddock beside the jumping field? It's such a lovely day it seems a shame for her to be inside and we're going to be very busy until mid afternoon."

Rosie said goodbye to her mum and then she and Milly untacked Angel and put her out in the small daytime paddock by the jump field.

"We should groom the ponies who are going to be used in the pony morning," said Milly. "The little ones are supposed to groom them before they ride but it always takes them forever just to do one small bit. I hope you don't mind grooming."

"I love it!" Rosie said with a smile.

*

The morning flew by. When the children arrived for the lead-rein pony morning they were each given a pony to look after and assigned a helper.

After riding in the school, the riders had a stable management lesson and then they went out on a hack and came back and played some gymkhana games. At lunchtime, they were collected and relative peace descended on the yard.

Hayley went out, leaving Kate in charge. Milly and Rosie took their packed lunches outside and sat on a bank, overlooking Angel's paddock. Angel was grazing contentedly in the sun and Rosie's heart swelled with love as she watched her cropping at the grass. When she and Milly had finished their food they lay back and chatted. They were just talking about how weird it was going to be starting secondary school when they heard voices in the jumping field.

Helena and Jo were bringing Jo's horse into the field. He was a bright bay with a small white star called Pasco. Rosie saw Angel lift her head from the grass and watch as Jo rode Pasco round. Jo was a very good rider. She hardly moved in the saddle even when Pasco bucked a few times.

"Does Jo go in shows?" Rosie asked curiously.

"Yes, she does a lot of showjumping," said Milly. "Helena is desperate to have a horse so she can go with her. Mum and Dad said that if she keeps working here and getting good grades at school they'll get one on loan for her for her fourteenth birthday in the summer."

Rosie glanced at her. "Won't you be jealous?"

Milly grinned. "No. If they get one for her then they'll have to get one for me when I'm fourteen too!"

They watched as Jo cantered Pasco over a few showjumps. He cleared them easily. Then she headed off round the field. There were cross-country fences around the outside and then some built in the hedges between the fields. But to stop the horses jumping over them when they were not supposed to each one had a removable extra bar fixed over the top. Each cross-country fence had a low and a high option. Some of the high options were massive – obviously meant just for Hayley and her eventers. Jo jumped round all the smaller fences.

"She shouldn't be doing that," said Milly, frowning. "We're not allowed to jump the cross-country fences unless Hayley's giving us a lesson."

Rosie watched slightly anxiously but Pasco flew over them all. Jo rode over to Helena and got off so she could have a go.

Helena rode Pasco round the show jumps. She wasn't quite as confident as Jo and Pasco faltered a few times. He got too close to the wall and knocked out some bricks and then knocked the gate down too but after that he collected himself and jumped cleanly around the rest. Jo called her over. She had a grin on her face. The two girls had a conversation that Rosie and Milly couldn't hear. Jo gestured to one of the cross-country jumps. There was a small telegraph pole on one side and an enormous tiger trap fence on the other.

"What's going on?" said Rosie curiously.

"I don't know." Milly frowned. "Maybe Helena's going to jump the cross-country fences like Jo did. Oh, she really shouldn't. She'll be in so much trouble if anyone sees."

Angel had gone to the fence and

was staring at the girls and Pasco. She stamped a hoof anxiously and looked back at Rosie.

Jo had her arms folded and a challenging look on her face. Uneasy shivers ran down Rosie's back. Helena cantered Pasco round to the cross-country jump Jo had pointed at. Her face was pale but determined.

Helena rode Pasco straight towards the massive tiger trap. It was a triangular fence with a huge ditch in the middle.

"What's she doing? She's not going to jump that is she? No way!" exclaimed Milly, jumping up and grabbing Rosie's arm as Helena sat back and kicked. Angel whinnied anxiously again. Milly's fingers dug into Rosie's skin but Rosie barely felt them as she watched Helena urging Pasco on. He hesitated as he approached the enormous fence. She kicked and he leapt forwards. She was mad. It was huge….

Rosie saw the brave horse lengthen his stride, saw his ears prick and then he took off. Her hands flew to her mouth. If he didn't clear it, he could end up falling, maybe breaking a leg or hurting Helena.

There was a moment when he was suspended in the air and the world seemed to stand still and then Pasco landed safely on the other side. Jo whooped as Helena cantered over.

Rosie turned to Milly, her heart hammering in her chest. "I can't believe she just did that!"

"It was another dare!" said Milly furiously. "He could have fallen. He could have really hurt himself – and her."

Abandoning their lunchboxes, she ran down the hill to the jumping field. Rosie followed her.

Helena spotted them and waved. Her cheeks were flushed with excitement. "Did you see that? Jo dared me to jump the tiger trap and I did!"

"Don't say it like it's something to be proud of!" Milly exploded. "What if he'd fallen?"

"I knew he wouldn't," said Jo.

"I'm going to tell Mum and Dad what you just did and about Jo going into the field yesterday and…"

"If you tell them, I'll never speak to you again," interrupted Helena. She pointed at her sister. "And when you come to Riverside I'll make your life a misery. Jo and I will get all of year nine to bully you. You're not to tell."

"You have to say you'll stop doing the dares then," said Milly.

They glared at each other for a long moment and then Helena shrugged. "All right, whatever. We'll stop doing the dares." Her eyes met Jo's and Rosie was sure she saw her wink.

"Yeah, course we'll stop," Jo said, smirking. "Come on, Helena. Let's leave the munchkins and take Pasco in. Hayley will be back soon."

Rosie and Milly watched them go.

"Do you think they really are going to stop?" Rosie said slowly.

Milly took a breath, slowly simmering down. "No."

"So what are you going to do?" Rosie said.

"I don't know. I haven't got any proof. If I tell anyone, Helena will just say I'm lying."

Rosie thought hard. "How about we follow them and if we catch them doing another dare we could even try to take a photo of them with your phone so you've got proof."

"You mean we spy on them?" said Milly.

Rosie nodded.

Milly grinned. "I like it!" she said and, lifting her hand, she clapped Rosie's in a high-five.

CHAPTER NINE

Rosie rode Angel up to Orchard Stables every day after that. She loved helping with the ponies, having lessons, hanging out with Milly and, most of all, just being with Angel. She liked it best when Hayley or Kate took them out on a hack with the other helpers and they got the chance to canter through the fields and up the hills.

Angel would leap forward with

her ears pricked and Rosie could feel the happiness surging through her. Leaning forward like a jockey, she forgot about everything else, losing herself in the wonderful beating rhythm of Angel's hooves.

Even hacking up to Orchard Stables every morning with her mum was fun. She loved having time to talk, just the two of them, and she was sure her mum was enjoying it too because one day, when her dad offered to walk her up there, her mum turned him down.

"It's our Rosie, Mum and Angel time, isn't it?" she said, giving Rosie a smile.

Rosie nodded and smiled back.

Her dad laughed. "Well, I wouldn't want to interfere with that! I like it that you two get some special time together." He patted Angel and ruffled her mane. Rosie exchanged a look with her mum – was her dad actually starting to come round to the idea that ponies weren't just nuisances?

In the evenings, Rosie would spend time grooming Angel and cleaning her tack. She liked to sit on an upturned bucket in Angel's field and clean her tack while the sun went down and Angel grazed beside her. It was their special time together, when it was just the two of them. Every day, Rosie felt like she understood

Angel a little bit more. Sometimes when Angel looked at her, Rosie felt like she could almost read her thoughts and although Angel was always friendly with everyone, Rosie knew she had a special soft whinny that she only used when it was Rosie walking towards her.

Rosie emailed lots of pictures of Angel to Alice – along with pictures of the lambs and some of Orchard Stables and Milly.

"Milly looks really nice," Alice emailed back. *"I'd really like to meet her."*

Rosie was determined that would happen as soon as Alice got home. Milly was just as keen to meet Alice too and she had plans for a party where Alice and Rosie could meet her friends from school. Some of them were going to the same secondary school as Alice.

"It would be brilliant if we could all hang round together," said Milly, who seemed to like making new friends as much as Rosie did. "And they can all moan together about how boring we are when we talk about horses!"

Milly's mum asked if Rosie wanted to come over for a sleepover the night before the Easter Egg hunt and when Helena heard their plans, she offered to let Angel stay in one of the fields overnight so Rosie could go straight to the stables in the morning without having to go home first. It sounded so much fun! Rosie couldn't wait!

On the day before the Easter Egg hunt, Rosie packed her suitcase so that her mum could drop it to Milly's house later on. "I'm looking forward to this barbecue tomorrow," Mrs Collington said. "Dad is going to come too. It'll be great to meet everyone you talk about."

"I'm looking forward to the Easter Egg hunt," said Rosie. "I bet Angel loves it!"

When Rosie rode on to the yard that morning, she found Hayley bathing one of Fudge's front legs. Milly was holding Fudge and watching in concern.

"Is Fudge OK?" Rosie asked, leading Angel over.

"She's got an overreach," said Hayley, pointing out a crescent-shaped wound just above Fudge's hoof. Angel touched her nose to Fudge's and snorted. Fudge whickered.

"How did she do it?" Rosie asked.

"I'm not sure – ponies get cuts like this when their back hoof cuts into their front leg. It sometimes happens when they're galloping or jumping but it wouldn't normally happen in the field. Not with a lazy pony like Fudge who hardly ever canters round."

"Maybe she got it yesterday when she was being ridden?" said Milly.

"No. Either Kate or I would have noticed it. She must have done it in the field," said Hayley. "Her coat's quite sweaty so it looks like she was galloping round for some reason." She sprayed some purple disinfectant spray on to the wound and put Fudge's leg down. "She'll have to stay in a stable and rest until it's healed. Hopefully it shouldn't take more than a few days."

"Do you want me to put her in a stable?" Milly offered.

"Yes please." Hayley handed Fudge's leadrope to Milly and started repacking the first aid kit. Milly led

Fudge into the pony barn. Rosie followed her with Angel.

Helena came out of one of the stables with a wheelbarrow. Fudge sidestepped away from her and put her ears back. Rosie looked at her in surprise. Fudge was normally a very friendly pony.

"What are you doing bringing Fudge in, Milly?" Helena asked, stopping with the wheelbarrow. "She isn't needed for lessons today. It's her day off."

"She'll be having more than one day off," said Milly. "She's hurt her front leg. Look. It's an overreach. Hayley said she must have done it by galloping about in the field."

111

"Galloping in the field?" For a fleeting moment, Rosie thought she saw an anxious look flash through Helena's eyes.

"Yes, silly pony," said Milly, patting Fudge's neck.

Helena bit her lip. "How badly hurt is she?"

"Hayley said she just needs a few days off. She'll be better soon."

Helena breathed out a sigh. "Phew."

Rosie frowned. That was an odd thing to say.

Helena caught her eye. "I mean it's really good she's not seriously injured," she said quickly. "That would be awful."

She picked up the wheelbarrow handles and hurried away. Rosie watched her go, unease prickling down her spine. There had been something very strange about Helena's reaction. But she couldn't have had anything to do with Fudge's injury, could she?

*

Half an hour later when Jo arrived, Rosie saw Helena drag her off to a quiet corner beside the muckheap. She watched from the water tap as Helena spoke quickly to Jo. She seemed agitated. Jo seemed to be calming her down. What was going on? Whatever it was, Jo seemed to shrug it off and started walking towards the pony barn with Helena beside her.

"Just chill," Rosie heard Jo saying as she got closer. "We'll make sure it doesn't happen again when it's your turn." She grinned. "You've got to do it or I win the game." Suddenly she caught sight of Rosie watching. "What are you looking at, Dumbo?"

"Nothing." Rosie quickly focused on the water bucket. But as Helena and Jo walked on, her thoughts raced. What had that conversation been about? A thought gradually formed in her mind making her eyes widen. Maybe Helena and Jo had been chasing the ponies around and making them gallop as part of some new dare. Maybe that was how Fudge had got injured? They hadn't done any dares since Helena had jumped Pasco as far as Rosie knew but perhaps this was the latest one.

"We'll make sure it doesn't happen again when it's your turn." Jo's words echoed ominously in Rosie's thoughts. She didn't like the sound of that at all.

*

"Jo said what? Tell me again – everything," whispered Milly. Rosie had had to wait until the morning lessons had started and it was quieter on the yard before they could speak in private. She had dragged Milly to Angel's paddock so they could talk without being overheard.

Rosie repeated the snatch of conversation while Angel stood between them. "I think they did something that made Fudge get that overreach. Helena acted really weird when you told her about it. Do you think they might have been chasing the ponies for some kind of dare?"

"I wouldn't put it past them," said Milly. "From now on we watch their every move. I'm going to get evidence and tell Mum. This has to stop."

Angel snorted. "Angel agrees," said Rosie. She patted Angel's neck. She knew Milly didn't want to tell tales and she didn't either but if ponies were getting injured they couldn't keep quiet, something definitely had to be done.

The rest of the day the helpers were all kept busy grooming, sweeping yards and poo-picking the fields. Everyone – even the older ones – was excited about the Easter Egg hunt.

When all the riding school work was done, they took the tack cleaning equipment out into the sun. Angel watched over the gate as Milly and Rosie settled down a little way off from the others and chatted about the next day and which team would be fastest at the Easter Egg hunt. *I hope it's me and Milly,* Rosie thought.

They had just finished cleaning

their saddles when Jo called over. "Hey, Midget. I need the silver polish."

Milly ignored her.

"Midget!"

The next second a sopping wet sponge sailed through the air. It hit Magpie's saddle before bouncing on to Angel's leaving dirty wet marks.

"Jo!" Kate said crossly. "Be careful."

"Whoops," Jo said, her eyes wide. "Sorry, my hand just slipped."

Kate rolled her eyes at her.

"It *did,*" Jo insisted with a giggle. She came over and got the metal polish. "Sorry, munchkins," she said with a smirk.

Rosie felt anger stir deep inside her and Milly looked like she was about to explode but there was nothing they could do but re-clean the saddles.

They finished before the others and put their tack away. Then Milly went to fetch Magpie and Rosie went to fetch Angel. They wanted to bath them so both ponies would be clean for the morning.

Angel had been watching the tack cleaning from her paddock. She whickered as Rosie walked over to her. She hoovered up some pony treats and then Rosie slipped her headcollar on.

"That pony is so cute," said Olivia, one of the teenagers, as Rosie led

Angel past them.

Rosie glowed.

"Just adorable," said Olivia's friend, Poppy. "You're so lucky, Rosie. I'd have loved a pony like Angel when I was your age."

Just then something seemed to startle Angel. She shied and her back leg caught the tack-cleaning bucket that was beside Jo. It fell over, the water splashing all over Jo's jodhpurs. Jo shrieked.

Rosie gasped. "Sorry!"

"I'm soaking!" Jo cried.

"I'm really sorry," said Rosie although she was giggling inside. "I don't know why she did that."

Kate grinned. "Maybe her hooves

just slipped."

All the older girls apart from Jo burst out laughing. "Thanks, guys!" Jo said crossly.

Rosie led Angel to the hitching rail and hugged her. "You did that on purpose, didn't you?" she whispered.

Angel blinked at her smugly.

Rosie giggled. "Jo deserved it." She hugged her. "Oh, Angel, I have a feeling she and Helena planning something. I hope it's not another stupid dare." She kissed Angel's nose. "If you see something, please will you try and tell me. Milly and I have to stop them before someone gets seriously hurt."

CHAPTER TEN

Rosie loved staying with Milly. The house wasn't very big but there was a lovely happy feel to it. Milly's little sister, Abigail, was very cute and Milly's mum and dad were very welcoming. Thankfully, Jo and Helena disappeared upstairs, leaving Milly and Rosie alone.

After tea, Rosie and Milly went up to Milly's room to play Horse Monopoly. It wasn't very big but Rosie liked it. It had bunk beds with duvets covers that had horses on and a big picture of a rearing horse on one wall. Best of all, it looked out over the field where Angel was staying that night. She and Milly had walked back to the house through the field and Angel had followed them all the way to the fence between the field and Milly's garden. When they'd climbed over it, she'd watched them go into the house.

She and Milly were halfway through the game when Rosie heard whinnying coming from the field. She looked at Milly. "Do you hear that?"

"What?"

Rosie went to the window. It was open a crack. She pushed it open more and then they both heard it – a pony whinnying over and over again.

"It's Angel," Rosie said.

"How do you know?" said Milly.

Rosie couldn't explain it. She just knew she'd know Angel's whinny anywhere. She looked out of the window but it was dusk outside now and she couldn't see the field very well. "She doesn't usually whinny like that," she said uneasily, remembering what she had said to Angel earlier. Maybe Angel was trying to tell her something. "I'd better check she's OK."

"She'll be fine," said Milly.

"No, something's the matter," Rosie insisted. "I know it is."

To her relief, Milly didn't argue. "OK, let's go to the field and check on her."

They slipped out through the back door. Angel was trotting up and down by the fence, still whinnying.

"What's the matter, girl?" said Rosie, climbing over. She went to stroke her but to her surprise, Angel moved away. She walked purposefully across the field. Rosie followed her. "Angel, come back."

But Angel didn't stop. She headed for the gate that led into the next field. Rosie broke into a run but Angel started to trot. Rosie's heart started to beat faster. She was sure Angel wanted her to follow her. But why?

Milly ran after Rosie. "What's she doing? Angel's never hard to catch. Why's she being...?" She broke off. "Who's that?"

They both listened. Faint voices were coming from the next field – the field where Hayley's eventers, Max and Solo, and the three youngsters were kept.

Rosie stiffened and put a finger to her lips. Milly nodded, understanding. They had to be quiet and find out what was going on. There shouldn't be voices in the field at this time of night.

They ran silently up to the gate. Angel whickered anxiously. As they joined her, Rosie caught her breath. The field was large but on the far side of it she could see two shadowy figures standing beside Solo, Hayley's best eventer. She and Milly exchanged alarmed looks.

Rosie sensed Milly was thinking the same as she was. Solo was worth a lot of money. These people must be trying to steal him. If that was the case, they had to do something...

Just then one of the figures started unbuckling the front of Solo's rug. "Come on, Helena. We don't want to be here all night." Jo's voice floated across the field.

"It's Helena and Jo!" Milly hissed.

Rosie's initial rush of relief was

quickly replaced by alarm. "What are they doing?" she said, as Jo and Helena took off Solo's rug. But even as she spoke, she guessed.

It has to be a dare. Maybe they were going to chase Solo round the field like they had chased Fudge? But why were they removing his rug?

"Are you going to get on him then?" she heard Jo say.

"I need a leg up," Helena said. "He's massive."

Rosie's blood froze. Oh no. They weren't going to *chase* Solo; they were going to *ride* him! Angel nudged her anxiously with her nose.

"The idiots!" hissed Milly in dismay.

Jo gave Helena a leg up. She landed on Solo's back. "I feel really high up!" she said, with a giggle.

"Least he's got boots on so he can't hurt his legs like Fudge," said Jo.

Rosie frowned but then realized what she meant. Solo was always turned out with protective boots on his legs so that he wouldn't hurt himself if he did gallop round.

"You don't have to gallop him like I did with Fudge," Jo went on. "We don't want Hayley finding him sweaty in the morning. Just trot him once round the field. That's your dare."

"OK. You're on." Helena held the

leadrope like a single rein and touched her heels to Solo's chestnut sides. "Trot on, Solo."

Solo looked surprised but did as she asked, breaking into a slow jog trot.

"We've got to stop them!" Milly turned Rosie. "This is crazy!" She reached for the bolt on the gate.

"Wait," hissed Rosie, grabbing her arm and stopping her. "If you run in there now, it might startle Solo and make him gallop off." Angel whickered unhappily. "Look, it might be OK," Rosie went on. "Hopefully she'll just trot him round and then get off."

Just then, Jo called out. "You're

hardly trotting at all. Go a bit faster!"

Helena kicked Solo. He sped up. "He's really bouncy!" she gasped. She let the leadrope go slack as she struggled to hang on.

The other four horses started to trot after Solo. As he got further away from them they broke into a canter. Hearing their hooves behind him, he started to canter too.

"They're going to stampede, Rosie!" Milly gasped. "It's why Hayley says we must never ride in the fields. Oh, stop, Helena, please stop!" she said in an agonized whisper.

Helena was pulling frantically on the leadrope but Solo barely seemed to feel her. He started to gallop, his giant strides eating up the ground as he charged down the field with the other horses behind him.

"Helena!" cried Milly, opening the gate.

The second Milly unlatched the gate, Angel plunged forward, almost knocking her over. She cantered into the field.

"No, Angel! No!" cried Rosie, running after her. "If you join in you'll make it worse!"

But Angel cantered away from her. The five horses were now galloping down the field straight towards the hedge at the bottom.

Milly started to sprint across the

field towards them, waving her arms. Rosie realized she was planning on running in front of the horses to try and stop them. She raced after her. "Milly! Be careful!"

"Stop!" Milly shrieked.

Helena was hanging on desperately to Solo's mane but she was starting to lose her grip and slip to one side.

The horses saw the end of the field approaching and to Rosie's relief they started to slow down from a gallop to a canter. A couple of them fell back into a trot. Helena took advantage of the slower pace to right herself and tug at Solo's leadrope. She turned his head towards the hedge at the bottom. Rosie realized she was trying to use it to stop him so she could get off.

But her plan went wrong. Solo's ears pricked as he saw the large cross-country jump that was in the middle of the hedge. His eyes locked on to it and his pace increased again.

Rosie heard Milly cry out. "He's going to jump it!"

Rosie's heart was in her mouth. He couldn't! He mustn't! There was the extra bar across the top making it even higher than usual but Milly had once told her Solo never stopped at a fence. For a moment everything seemed to go into slow motion. Rosie saw Helena's terrified face as she realized what was happening. She saw Solo's muscles bunch as he prepared to take off and then suddenly, out of nowhere Angel galloped in front of him, cutting between him and fence. Solo stopped abruptly, pulling up short so he didn't crash into the palomino pony. The sudden stop sent Helena flying over his head.

Rosie and Milly raced over to where she lay on the ground. Jo was now running down the field, the rug abandoned on the floor. Helena lay still. Angel had wheeled round and trotted over to her. She stopped beside the girl on the ground, lowering her head and gently blowing on her hands and face.

"Helena! Are you all right?" cried Milly.

Helena pushed herself into a sitting position. She was pale with shock. Rosie and Milly crouched down beside her, their breath coming in gasps. Solo had wandered off to graze with the other horses, no worse the wear for his gallop.

"Oh Helena." Milly hugged her sister. "I thought you were going to die."

Tears welled up in Helena's eyes. "That was so scary. I thought he wasn't going to stop. He would have jumped it if Angel hadn't galloped in front of him."

Rosie reached up to stroke her pony's shoulder. Angel was watching everything.

"Helena, are you all right?" Jo panted. She looked almost as pale as Helena and for once she wasn't laughing.

"My wrist. It really hurts." Helena tried to move her left hand but caught her breath in pain. "But the rest of me's OK." Jo helped her to her feet.

Milly's relief turned to anger. "What were you thinking of, Helena? Why did you even consider riding Solo like that?"

"It was a dare," Helena said.

"It was the most stupid dare I've ever seen," blazed Milly. "That's it.

I'm telling Mum!"

"No! Please don't," gasped Helena. "If you do she won't ever let me have a horse on loan. I know she won't. Please, Milly. I'll do anything you want. I'll stop doing the dares, I promise."

"Yeah, I don't think we should do this any more," said Jo.

"Too right you shouldn't!" snapped Milly. She looked from one to the other. They both looked shocked and upset. She took a breath, her anger fading slightly. "OK then. I won't tell. If you really mean you'll stop."

"We will. I promise," said Helena.

"What are you going to say about

your wrist?" said Milly.

"I don't know. I'll say we were messing round in the garden and I fell. I think I'm going to have to go to hospital. It really hurts."

"You won't be able to ride in the Easter Egg hunt tomorrow," Milly said.

"I know," said Helena.

They were all silent for a moment and Rosie wondered if the others were thinking the same as she was – that if Angel hadn't stopped Solo, if he'd actually tried to do the jump, Helena might not have been riding ever again.

"I'll put Solo's rug back on," said Jo, clearing her throat.

Milly and Rosie started walking back with Helena in the direction of home. Angel walked beside them, calm now. Luckily none of the other mares had come through the open gate.

"I saw you running towards me when Solo was galloping down the field Milly," said Helena quietly. "What were you doing?"

"I wanted to try and stop the horses – I thought they might slow down if I ran in front of them," said Milly.

"That was really brave," said Helena. "You could have got trampled."

Milly shrugged. "You'd have done

it for me."

Helena gave a small nod. "Yeah. I would." They smiled at each other for once.

"I wouldn't have got there in time anyway," said Milly. "Luckily Angel did."

Helena stroked Angel and smiled at Rosie. "She's amazing." Angel looked at her through her long forelock. "If she hadn't whinnied to you and got you to come out and then galloped in front of Solo like that then..." Her words trailed off.

Rosie put her arm over Angel's neck. "You're the best pony in the world, aren't you?"

Angel looked at her happily. *Oh*

yes, her eyes seemed to say. *I am!*

CHAPTER ELEVEN

"Over here, Milly! Quick! I've found another egg!" shrieked Rosie as she halted Angel beside an oak tree in the woods.

Milly raced over on Magpie. "How many have we got now?"

"Nine," said Rosie. "Just one more to get!"

It was the next morning and although the events from the night before had faded, Rosie knew she would never forget them. She hoped

Jo and Helena felt the same. Luckily, Helena's mum had believed her when she said she had fallen over in the garden. She'd taken Helena to hospital where the doctor had told her she had sprained her wrist but not broken it. It was now bandaged up and she was watching the hunt from back at the stables.

Rosie took a little cut-out paper egg from the box underneath the big cardboard egg and scrambled back on to Angel. The idea of the race was for the teams to find all ten painted cardboard eggs hidden throughout the stables' fields and woods. Every time they found one they collected a little mini paper egg and carried on.

The first team back with all ten mini eggs was going to be the winner.

She read out the final clue.

"Where horses get wet and sometimes riders do too

Look for an egg painted bright blue!"

Milly's eyes gleamed. "I bet the egg's by the water jump. Horses get wet when they jump in there and sometimes riders do if they fall off."

"To the water jump!" cried Rosie. Angel whinnied with excitement.

They galloped through the woods and out into the field. Angel surged ahead of Magpie, her ears pricked. Rosie could feel Angel's excitement matching her own. Bending low over Angel's neck, she let her gallop as fast as she wanted towards the water complex.

"Wait for me!" shrieked Milly.

Glancing round, Rosie saw Milly kicking frantically as Magpie galloped along behind. Grinning, Rosie slowed down for her friend. They cantered side by side until they reached the water jump. Milly had been right. There was a bright blue egg nailed to one of the poles. They had them all!

"Come on!"

They raced back to the stables. As they approached the finish line they saw Helena there with Jo and Milly's parents. Seeing Milly and Rosie galloping towards the finish, she and

Jo whooped loudly.

"Come on, Milly! Come on, Rosie!" Since the night before they'd stopped calling them by mean nicknames. Rosie wasn't sure their friendliness would last but right now she was enjoying it. Jo had even helped her plait Angel's tail that morning so that it looked extra nice.

"Come on, Angel," Rosie urged. Angel responded. She increased her pace and raced over the finish line with Magpie just behind her.

Rosie heard more cheering and looked round to see her Mum and Dad standing there. She tried to slow Angel down and catch her breath.

"You're first!" shouted Jo. "If

you've got all the eggs, you've won!"

And they had. Hayley counted them out and declared Milly and Rosie the winners. "You'll get your prize at the barbecue," she said. "Well done. Magpie and Angel can certainly both gallop fast. I'm starting a mounted games team for the Pony Club after Easter – do you think you might both be interested in joining?"

"Oh yes!" gasped Rosie and Milly.

Hayley smiled. "Great. Now go and cool those ponies off."

As Rosie led Angel away to wash her down, her happiness faded a notch as she realised something. She would only be able to do the mounted games team and carry on riding at Orchard Stables if her dad said she could keep Angel. "Oh, Angel," she whispered. "He can't send you back now!"

She was just tying Angel up when her mum and dad came over to her. "That was fantastic!" said her mum. "You and Milly were so fast."

"Angel was amazing," said Rosie, wrapping her fingers in Angel's silky mane. She bit her lip and looked at her dad. She couldn't wait any longer. She had to ask him if he had made up his mind about Angel. "Dad..." She took a deep breath. "About Angel. Have you... have you made up your mind? Can I keep her?"

He frowned and Rosie's heart sank. "Hmm," he said. "Well, you know what I feel about ponies..."

Rosie felt tears well in her eyes. He was going to send Angel back!

"Pete, don't be mean!" her mum said, elbowing him with a smile. "Stop teasing."

Rosie stared between the two of them. Her dad's face broke into a broad grin. "Oh, all right then. Yes, Rosie, you can keep her."

"Really?" Rosie gasped.

"Yes," her dad said, ruffling Angel's mane. "I'm still not a fan of ponies but there's definitely something special about this one. She can stay."

Rosie felt like she was exploding with happiness. "Oh, Angel," she cried, wrapping her arms round Angel's neck and hugging her hard. Suddenly her head was filled with the thoughts of the summer ahead of them with hacks, lessons, jumping and mounted games. "Did you hear that? You can stay!"

*

At the barbecue, Hayley presented Rosie and Milly with two massive Easter eggs. The other helpers all got smaller Easter eggs. Some of the dads including Rosie and Milly's dads started cooking the sausages and burgers while everyone else sat around, talking and laughing.

Rosie and Milly's mums were chatting and Milly was lying on her back in the sun. Rosie wrapped her arms around her knees and she looked at the little paddock by the jump field where Angel was contentedly cropping at the grass. It had been a wonderful day.

And it's all thanks to Angel, she thought. *If she hadn't trotted off that day I'd never have come to Orchard Stables or met Milly; I'd never have made so many new friends or had so much fun. And we might not have saved Helena.*

As if Angel sensed Rosie was thinking about her, she lifted her head. Rosie got up and went down to the gate. Angel walked over to meet her. "You know, I think you trotted down here on purpose that day," Rosie whispered, stroking her silky mane. "You knew it would be a good thing to do, didn't you?"

Angel looked at her with her wise dark eyes. Rosie wrapped her arms around her. "Dad's right," she said. "There really *is* something very, very special about you."

As she hugged her she felt as if a cloud of love was surrounding them, holding them together.

"You're my Angel-pony, aren't you?" Rosie said happily.

Angel snorted in reply.

Hello From Linda

Thank you for reading *Best Friends*. I really hope you enjoyed it because I certainly loved writing it! It's only the start of Angel and Rosie's adventures - they've got a whole load more fun and excitement to come so look out for more books about them in the future!

I had my first book published back in 1999 and since then I have written over 200 books. Some of my best-known series are *My Secret Unicorn, Stardust, Skating School* and *Best Friends Bakery* as well as *Sophie and the Shadow Woods* written with Lee Weatherly.

I live in a village in Leicestershire, England with my husband, three children, two dogs and two ponies. One of my ponies is called Angel and she is just like Angel in this story. She's a 13hh, palomino Welsh pony who is very loving and kind, but who is also very greedy! If you would like to know more about Angel then check out www.aponycalledangel.com.You'll find photos and competitions and lots of fun Angel info on there!

You can find out more about my other books on my author website: www.lindachapmanauthor.co.uk.If you would like to contact me then you will find the details on both websites about how you can get in touch. Happy Reading!

Love Linda x

COMING SOON...

A Pony Called Angel

Fun and Games

Find out what Rosie and Angel get up to next! What happens when they start training for the MOUNTED GAMES team? What will MILLY and ALICE think of each other when they meet? And are a rival team really trying to SABOTAGE Rosie and Angel's chances in the championships? One thing's for sure there are lots of fun and games ahead!

Publishing Summer 2016 on Amazon – look out for it!

20879691R00091

Printed in Great Britain
by Amazon